C. Visalini

Your Love Is Like Christmas

First Published in November 2020

ISBN: 978-93-5427-053-6

BLUEROSE PUBLISHERS

www.bluerosepublishers.com

info@bluerosepublishers.com

+91 8882 898 898

Cover Design:

Jasleen Ashta

Typographic Design:

Ilma Mirza

Distributed by: BlueRose, Amazon, Flipkart, Shopclues

Content

Chapter 1 ____ 1
Toxic relationship ____ 1
Chapter 2 ____ 3
Emily's birthday ____ 3
Chapter 3 ____ 5
Hate him ____ 5
Chapter 4 ____ 6
My dream ____ 6
Chapter 5 ____ 9
The trouble makers ____ 9
Chapter 6 ____ 12
Our first fight ____ 12
Chapter 7 ____ 16
Is my client really not guilty? ____ 16
Chapter 8 ____ 20
The first trial ____ 20
Chapter 9 ____ 23
Investigation ____ 23
Chapter 10 ____ 25
The second trial ____ 25
Chapter 11 ____ 29
Long- distance relationship ____ 29
Chapter 12 ____ 31
Paris I'm in love ____ 31
Chapter 13 ____ 34
Unexpected love ____ 34

Chapter 1

Toxic relationship

Todd asked me to come to a fancy restaurant. I was so happy because he never takes me out. He never spends any money or time on me. I got ready and went there. He was waiting for me outside the restaurant. He was nervous. We both walked inside the restaurant. He said he wanted to talk to me about something serious. We settled down very comfortably. A s soon as I sat down, he said he wanted a break. I was shocked and confused. I asked, ' From what do you want a break?' He answered in a harsh tone that he wanted a break from this relationship. I was angry. I asked him why this all of a sudden.

'Y ou only read books and newspapers.'

' I like the feel of paper in my hands and I always want to learn something new.'

'You do n't even use your phone. You only use your phone for calling. Y ou don't have any apps o n your phone. How can I be with someone who is not there o n any social media?! It's like I'm dating a grandma.'

'W ell, I don't want to get distracted from my studies.'

Y ' ou are a little old for me.'

' I am younger than you! And you're not so perfect either, Todd. You take pictures of everything, everywhere instead of enjoying the moment! There are more important things in the world.'

'L ike you know everything t hat's happening. You always study and spend more time i n the library than spending time with me.'

' Hey, you know that I want to become a lawyer! I should work hard to get good grades in my law exams. Wait a minute... you have never taken me anywhere nice. Did you bring me here just so I wouldn't make a scene?'

'Y es, because I knew you wouldn't do anything crazy in public. You don't even know how to speak to my friends. You never come to see any of my matches.'

'L ook, don't act like you're a perfect boyfriend. You never kno w when my birthday is, you always put me down in front of your friends, you always discourage me and you don't support me with my dreams. Your friends are d***heads, they never kno w how to behave in front of a girl .

'So you know what Todd?

'We are OVER!

'You're the worst. Have a nice life, Todd.'

Chapter 2

Emily's birthday

My name is Bella. I'm 23 years old. My native city is Los Angeles. I never have any thoughts about my love life but I always believe that there will be someone who will mend my broken heart. I am focused on my career and my dreams. I spent my college life with my books. My best friend Emily was very supportive. I never went to any parties when my friends were enjoying college life. I stayed home studying and researching on my computer.

On October 2 , i t was Emily's birthday. She forced me to come to her birthday party at Exchange LA Club. I wasn't interested but I didn't want to hurt her so I went to her party. Everyone was busy drinking and dancing. I was so bored that I thought I would go back home. As I was o n the way to my home, I heard a deep , strong voice calling my name. I turned back and looked at him. He came near me with two girls who were busy hitting on him. He was tall with attractive blue eyes. H is eyes li t up when he smiled. He was drop- dead gorgeous. H e looked at me and winked. He asked me, ' A re you the nerdy girl in our college?' He was very sexy, charming, and drunk. He asked me ' A re you leaving the party this early? I f you stay, we could have some fun.' I said I was not his type and walked back home. He called my name again and asked me for my number with an amused smirk playing at his lips. Something twinkled in his eyes as I stared at him for a moment. I said I won't give my number to an anonymous person and I left .

Chapter 3

Hate him

The next day in college, I saw him again. H e winked at me with a smile o n his face. The little dimple on his face poked out when he smirked . *He is just a hot guy. Who cares?* I had a lot of other work to do. I decided that it was best to ignore him and go back to my class. I went back to class. I was busy preparing for my law exams. He was the exact opposite of me. H e played around without studying. He was good at sports. Many girls were hitting on him . He flirted with all girls, hooked up with random girls, and was partying and drinking . He always teased me. Wh er ever I went, he called me a nerd. He threw paper at me, pulled my chair while I was sitting, and mad e fun of me. I hated him so much. Time went on. I got good marks in my college. I got really good grades in my law exams. After graduation, I got my dream job in Munich.

Chapter 4

My dream

I took a flight from Los Angeles to Munich. I was very happy that I got a job in one of the best law firms in the world, but I couldn't see my parents before leaving Los Angeles. My parents were very busy as they travelled around the world for their business. I always tried staying in contact with them . I could only see them once or twice a year. My friend Emily came to the airport to see me. I said goodbye to her and went to Munich. I got a job at Law Resolve (one of the famous law firms in Germany). Law Resolve's shareholder was sweet but very strict when it came to work. His name was Mr Theo. The f irst few months working at Law Resolve were a bit difficult. N ew place, new surroundings, but then I got used to it. Beau was a good friend to me from the starting day of my work. He was a computer genius and a great hacker. I got a separate office. I n a few days, I got many clients. I started learning new things in each case. I was working as a criminal defence lawyer. S oon, I got a higher position in the law firm. Mr Theo said there was a huge case waiting for me and the client was one of his friends. He gave me the files regarding the case and said to me that in court, this case hasn't come yet but I should be prepared. In that file, there was not much in detail about my client. The next day, Mr Theo called me to his office and introduced me to Jake. He said that he would be my partner in my new case and I should share my office with him. I was shocked to see Jake. H e was the same guy who I had hated so much in college but now he was a little different. H e was well-dressed, calm, and his mannerisms had changed. I argued with Mr Theo that I could handle the case by myself and I can't share my office with Jake, but Mr Theo wasn't ready to listen to what I was saying. Jake and I worked together all day on the case in which my client was charged . We researched who our client was and f or what he was being charged. But we couldn't find what really happened without speaking to the client. Jake never spoke to me during work hours but after we completed the work, he started teasing me and said he missed our small fights. I n fact, even I missed them . Jake helped me a lot . He started reading books. I never saw him reading books in our college. Mr Theo called us both to his office. He invited us to come to his party and asked us to dress well because there were more rich people who were attending the party. Jake picked me up from his house as his house was on the next street. His native city was Munich so he knew every place in Munich. We went to the party. T here were many rich people attending it . I asked him to come with me for a drink. H e said he had stopped drinking so I went alone to get champagne. He was a dru nk ard in our college time but now... I drank only one glass of champagne. Jake and I started talking, having fun, and roaming around. We really enjoyed each other's company. The n ext day was Saturday, no work, so Jake took me to Marienplatz. T he view from it was beautiful. H e also took me to the English G arden. T he place was peaceful and full of greenery. We sat near the lake and spoke about his parents, his life. We had a lot of fun. During the week days, we worked and o n the weekend, we hu ng out together. He also took me to the Nymphenburg Palace, Munich Residenz , New Town H all, Lake Sta rnberg, and to the best restaurants in Munich. He always shared everything about his life with me but he always ignored my question whenever I asked him why he changed . He tried changing the topic or said that it's a dirty s ecret . We didn't get any idea about our new case . I researched day and night on the background of my client. I n the office, I fell down unconscious. Jake sprinkled water on my face. I came back to consciousness but I couldn't walk as I felt so weak. Jake carried me to his home, prepared and gave me dinner, and told me to sleep on the bed while he slept on the couch. The next morning, I felt very wea k. Jake took care of me and made me breakfast. T hen, he took me to the hospital. The doctor said that I was very wea k because I didn't sleep and eat well. H e gave me vitamin tablets and told me to take rest. Jake took me back home. I couldn't sleep because my thoughts were on the case. Jake took me to a mountain- like place from where the whole city looked small. The view was amazing. H e walked very close to me and he ld my hand. W e were enjoying the moment. He came really close to me and was looking at me. I could smell his woody citrus scent and feel his warm breath on my neck. He took my hand and pulled me towards him. T hen he put his hand on my hips. I could feel butterflies in my stomach. Our eyes locked for a moment . H e suddenly realized it and took his hand away from my hips. I immediately longed for his touch again. The ride home was awkward. H e did not speak a single word and neither did I . He dropped me back to my house and left without a good bye.

Chapter 5

The trouble makers

The next day, Jake called me to the nearest coffee shop. His tone was different as if something was scaring him. I got ready and went to the shop. He was nervously seated. I sat down with him and I asked him whether something was wrong. He said there was a g a la tomorrow. I t was an important g al a for Mr Theo. There would be more business meetings at the g a la and Mr Theo invited us. I t would also be helpful if we interact with other people there . We could get more clients for our law firm but he cannot go . I asked him why. He said that there is a secret about him that I don't know. I was very curious to know what he was going to say . He said, ' I was a player in college because I never believed in love . In high school, I dated a girl but she cheated on me with my best friend Channel because he was richer than me. From that day, I thought that girls only love a guy for money. I really loved her very much but after this betrayal, I never spoke to either of them . I haven't seen them in ages but now they are coming to the g a la. He put up a story that he and my ex- girlfriend are going to the g a la . I can't face them.' I felt really bad for Jake . I told him to face his fear and I promised him that no matter what, I would be by his side. With a lot of hesitation, he asked me to come. I got ready to go to the g a la. He was waiting for me outside my house. I opened the door. He was wearing a black suit that he looked very attractive in . His face was shocked when I opened the door. I walked closer to him and called out his name. H e didn't respond. 'Jake, Jake, Jake!' H e was sta ring at me and after a few seconds, he said, 'B reath taking.' I giggled. He coughed and said, 'You look very pretty.' We drove to the g a la. A s soon as we got to the g a la, there was one guy who was disturbing me and he pulled my hand. Jake got very angry and hit him. It was the first time I had seen Jake this angry. I stopped Jake and pulled him away. I knew he was protective of me but I didn't know that he would get this angry. I tried to cool him down. I teased him and he started laughing. We started towards the g a la dance floor and there was romantic music playing around. Jake asked , 'C an I have a dance with you?' I replied, 'Yes.' As we danced, the world seemed to stop. I felt like I was in a dream. I felt safe and complete in his arms. I found myself falling for him.

Jake said, 'You are truly beautiful, Bella. I am lucky to dance with you tonight.'

Suddenly, a guy came and called Jake . He had a harsh voice. He was a tall, rich- looking blonde guy. As soon as Jake saw him, the happiness in his face went away. The blonde guy introduced himself to me and said that his name was Channel. I figured out why Jake looked angry. He came with Jake's ex- girlfriend Grace. They both started making fun of Jake. Channel looked at me and said, 'Y ou are a pretty girl. Why are you roaming with this loser?' I looked at Channel and said, 'Y our friend is the most incredible person I've ever known. He is sweet, caring, and generous with me! Channel, you are the real loser. Y ou don't deserve a friend like this and Grace, you missed out on a treasure that you had. ' They both went back angrily.

Jake said, 'I can't believe you said that . You are amazing, Bella. Thank you.'

' It's nothing. You would've done the same ' replied Bella.

B oth of us didn't want that night to end. We went on a walk nearby. Jake heard the sound of waves. He took me to the beach. The beach was empty. When the moon rays fell on the ocean, it looked gorgeous . Jake removed his shirt and jumped inside the water. Looking at s hirtless Jake with a perfect body and muscles, I couldn't see any thing other than him . I turned back and I was scared whether anyone else could see us. Jake kept on calling me . He asked me to enter the water. I said that I didn't bring my swimsuit. H e asked me to remove my clothes, wear his shirt, and enter the sea. I hesitant ly asked him whether the water was cold. H e started laughing and making fun of me . I removed my dress, put on his shirt, and entered the water. The water was freezing cold. I started shivering. Jake pulled me closer. He was holding me in his arms, trying to warm me up. I cuddled against him, resting my head on his chest. I could feel his heart beating so fast. He bent down, resting his head against my shoulder. I could feel his warm breath down on my neck. His fingers started going up my cheeks. He cupped my face into his hands and started kissing me. His lips had a salty taste from the sea water. I t made me prickle. I wrapped my arm against his wet shoulder and kissed him back, more intensely. The kiss was intoxicating. It just felt right.

Chapter 6

Our first fight

We both knew what our job was. We had our own boundaries. We knew that when it wa s work, we should not get distracted. I was going through files day and night, collecting data and information about my clients . I asked Beau to help me and Jake was also researching about my clients. All the days working on this case drove me crazy . I couldn't get a clear picture without speaking to our client . I set a meeting with our client because our case was going to court in two months. I went to the nearby coffee shop to get coffee. I met Grace there and she threatened me to stay away from Jake . I just ignored her and bought my coffee . She got pissed. She pulled my hand and said that Jake was a murderer. I was shocked. I knew that Jake was hiding something from me but I never thought he would be a murderer. E ven after Grace said that to me, I thought that Jake couldn't be a murderer. I wanted to ask him what his dirty s ecret was but I didn't want to make him upset by asking that question. S o, I went to my office, fini shed my work, and went home . The n ext day, our receptionist said that there was an envelope in my office with no name. When I went there, I saw that the envelope was missing. I asked Jake whether he saw any envelope and he said no. The next day again, the receptionist said that there was an envelope on my table with my name, but when I checked, it was not there. I searched my office and it was not there. Jake said that there was no envelope in my place when he entered the office. A few weeks went by. E very day, the receptionist kept the envelope o n my table but when I looked, it was missing. I wanted to find who was really taking the envelope so the next day, I went to the office fast and hid behind the curtain. I saw the receptionist putting the envelope and Jake taking and hiding it. I got really angry at Jake but I calmed down myself . After Jake went out of the office, I came out. W hen Jake came inside, I again asked whether he saw any envelope and he said no. Jake never lied to me. I got really angry at him and scolded him very badly. I even called him a murderer. He didn't say anything. He went out of our office. As the week went by, I stopped talking to Jake and even he didn't speak to me. I started ignoring him. I went to ask Beau for help regarding my client's relative s but Beau asked me about the envelope. I didn't understand how Beau knew about the envelope. Then he started explaining to me that the letter was from someone who was involved in this case. Those letters were threatening letters. Jake and Beau tried to figure out who sent those letters but they couldn't. Jake didn't want me to get scared or disturbed because of the letters so he hid them . I felt ashamed of myself for the way I treated Jake. He was not doing anything wrong. I couldn't speak to Jake during office hours because he didn't come to our office. It was evening when I reached home. I started crying, looking at myself in the mirror. It was cloudy outside. I ran to Jake's home . I called out his name and knocked on the door. T here was no response but I could see the light in his room.

' Jake, please open the door. I know you're in there. I can see the light on... Please open the door. I need to talk to you.'

He came down with watery eyes. He spoke in a broken voice.

'W hat do you want, Bella? It's late, you should go to your home.'

'No, I have to say something to you.'

' I'm listening.'

'Look, I know that I hurt you with harsh words that I didn't even mean. I don't know why it took this long for me to understand how important you are in my life. I never understood how much you cared about me. I was scared to accept my feelings towards you. I don't want to know your past. I want you to be my present. I like you the way you are. I love you Jake. I am completely in love with you.'

' I wanted to tell you the reason why I completely changed. I hooked up with a girl many times. One day, she came and proposed to me. She was drunk and I was drunk too. I hurt her feelings very badly by saying that love doesn't exist. To prove her love feelings for me, she jumped from the window. I couldn't help her. I was fully drunk and unable to walk. She died in front of my eyes. She was Grace's friend . Grace always used to call me a murderer after that and I accepted my fault . The reason for her death was me. From that day, I stopped drinking. I always end up hurting someone I love or someone who loves me. Don't take that risk after knowing about me.'

Rain started pouring down.

'I'm willing to take a chance on you, Jake. The question is, are you?'

'W hy do you even ask?'

He crashed his lips on mine, giving me a hard thrusting kiss. The rain was pouring down our faces. His hands wandered on my soaked shirt. I felt the warmth in my body. I desperately needed this kiss to last long, maybe forever. I felt this is exactly what I wanted for my life time. The rain was very heavy. We ran inside his house. He looked at me with a smile on his face. He hugged me and said, 'S pending all these days without talking to you drove me crazy. I can't do this anymore. I want you, I want to be with you and I will never let you go, Bella.' We went to his room. We cuddled and slept because tomorrow we were going to meet our client so proper sleep was important.

Chapter 7

Is my client really not guilty?

The next day, we went to meet our client because, in three weeks, our case was going to the court for trial . Mr Cameron Dallas was our client. He was a young billionaire. He was arrested for attempt of murder. We asked why the police arrested him. He said, ' I own several factories and buildings all around the world. I have a special interest in art. I have many business deals with famous artists all around the world. I own an art gallery so the artists would make a business deal with me. Three weeks ago, I bought a master piece from Mr Elijah (the famous artist from New York). I kept the master piece in a special room. The room was very secured. The door would only open with my fingerprint and there were surveillance cameras, hidden cameras, and night vision cameras everywhere. The hidden camera could see everything even in fog and was recorded 24×7 . No one knew about these hidden cameras. The next day, I went to the art gallery with my business partners to show my new master piece. My business partners are really trustworthy. I took a maid with me to the room because, in the special room, there was a lot of dust . I took her with me to clean the room while I was making the deal with my partner. S he was 42 years old. Her name was Miss Ava. She has been sincere in this job for more than 15 years . She didn't have any family and she was in poverty. I offered her this job and she has always been loyal to me.

Ava, my partners, and I went to the special room to make a deal and to start a collaboration with their company. When we entered the room, Miss Ava asked for my permission and went to clean . We five people started to talk about business but none of the deals were satisfying. I was a bit confused. M y friend saw me and he asked me to show all the master pieces I have been collecting to the other partners so that they could get a clear view of how important that master piece is . I agreed with him. The five of us started walking. I showed them all my art collection and my master pieces and how lucky they would be to make a deal with me. It was going on well. S uddenly, there was smoke everywhere and I couldn't see anything. There was no noise. B ecause of the smoke, I started coughing. I heard some other people also coughing. After some time, I could hear a person coughing. I called out for them but no one responded. S oon, the smoke started disappearing. I could see someone lying down. I t was Miss Ava and someone had shot her even though I didn't hear any shooting sound. The entrance was open and my security guards were missing. I had seen the security when I was entering the room . I immediately called the police and said there was a murder. A fter hearing this, the police cut the call and came there within ten minutes. They didn't investigate anything, they just immediately arrested me . I told them that I was not the murderer but they didn't listen. T hey showed me a photo of me having a gun. I was scared. I contacted my advisor. H e is a retired lawyer. H e said that Law Resolve is the best law firm. I found out that my friend Theo is the head of the law firm and I asked him for help. I promise you that I am not a murderer.'

Jake asked, 'W ho are the people who entered the room with you? And what are their businesses?'

Mr Cameron said, 'The first one, Daniel, is an actor. H e is very rich and he likes art works. He buys many pictures from my art gallery. We have been doing business for three years.

'The second one, Jacob, is my friend. W e have been good friends since childhood. He helps me with all my business and sometimes, he even buys pictures from me.

'The third one, Lincoln, is a big shot and he has many criminal records but has never been involved in any sought after murder activity. H e does illegal business and small c rimes. I have been working with him for three years.

'The fourth one, Mathew, is similar to me . He owns several companies and has a big craze for art. He goes to different places and buys the best art works.'

I asked him 'D id you see any security when you were entering the room?'

He said, 'Y es, but when I came out, they were missing.'

The t ime was up so we came out and went to our office. B oth of us had many questions in our minds . The police inspector was not ready to help us. We knew the seriousness of this case. Jake came up with many questions. Why did they kill the maid? How can the police arrest without proper evidence? How did the police get that photo? I couldn't answer any of these questions because these were the same questions that I had been thinking about. We went to Daniel, Jacob, Lincoln, and Mathew's houses to investigate but all answers were the same. We asked them how they came out of the room but they said that the door was open. Mr Cameron had said that without his finger print, the door could not open. We went to meet his wife. She started crying soon after we started the enquiry. She didn't answer any of our questions. S he was begging us to prove that her husband was not guilty. We investigated more on this case. We worked all day and night. I suspected Mr Lincoln because he had a criminal record but we did not get any proof that Mr Lincoln was the murderer. After having conversations with Mr Cameron, we understood what exactly happened in the room. We got a little evidence to say that our client was not guilty and even Beau helped us.

Chapter 8

The first trial

We prepared all the evidence that we had been collecting for weeks. Jake and I got ready and went to the court. The plaintiff was sitting on the right side and as the defendant, we were sitting on the left side. The court reporters were sitting near the judge's seat. We all stood up when the judge entered the courtroom and when the bailiff said, ' A ll rise. ' Mr Cameron was standing in the box with folded hands and bowed head . The j udge came in, sat down, and explained to everyone what this trial was about. Mr Sawyer was our plaintiff.

He said, 'Y our honour, this is Mr Cameron. H e is being accused of attempt of murder. This is the evidence that he is the one who shot Miss Ava.'

He showed the photo of Mr Cameron with the gun in his hand.

The judge said, 'N ow, the defendant may speak.'

I stood up and showed another picture. This was of Daniel, Lincoln, Mathew, and Jacob holding a gun in his hand. Jake even showed the judge a picture of Mr Sawyer himself holding a gun in his hand. The judge and Mr Sawyer were shocked. The whole court room was confused.

Jake said, 'Y our honour, t his is fake evidence in this modern technology. Anyone can do photoshop. This picture of my client can't be taken as evidence. The police didn't investigate properly i n this case. We need to investigate I nspector Lucas .'

Inspector Lucas came.

I asked, 'Inspector Lucas, how did you know the correct address of the art gallery?'

The inspector said that it was my client who called him and told him the place. While investigating , Inspector Lucas didn't cooperate with us so Jake asked the DIG for help. Jake recorded the conversation of our client and I nspector Lucas. We showed the audio to the judge in which my client did not mention the address. Inspector Lucas then said, ' I checked the GPS. I asked the inspector. 'Y ou said that my client told you the address but now you are saying that you checked the GPS. To travel from the police station to the art gallery, it takes thirty minutes. How could you reach the art gallery in ten minutes?' The judge asked the plaintiff if they had any evidence other than the photo. They answered no. The judge asked how the inspector go t that photo. The plaintiff answered that the photo was taken from the surveillance camera. Jake got up and said that the camera room docs not give access to anyone except our client. The entrance system would have asked for the fingerprint.

Mr Sawyer said, 'I humbly request you to adjourn the proceedings to another day so that I can bring more evidence.'

The j udge said, ' There are two important things to be noted in this case. The first one is that the police department hasn't conducted a fair investigation. The s econd is that there is something between I nspector Lucas and this case. I hereby order to suspend I nspector Lucas and conduct enquiry. There will be another officer who will take up this case. The next hearing will be conducted next month.'

The first trial was over. We did a good job. The new officer taking the case was Eric. He was Jake's friend. He studied with Jake in high school . He helped us with the case.

Chapter 9

Investigation

The police started investigating more on this case. We could meet our client anytime with Eric's help. Jake asked permission from Mr Cameron to access the camera room. We couldn't take our client out so Jake used silicon gel to take our client's fingerprint. I got evidence after seeing Jake taking Mr Cameron's fingerprint. This must have been the same method for the culprit who opened the door. Jake and Beau went to the camera room to get evidence while Eric and I were investigating the case. We went to the art gallery to get evidence. W e saw many surveillance cameras . I asked the security, 'O n May 27 (the date on which the police arrested Mr Cameron) why was everyone missing?' The security guard said that it was Mrs Cameron who asked him to come to her mansion. Eric asked about the other guards. H e replied that everyone was given other duties by Mr Cameron's PA . We went to the PA's house. I remembered that on that day, the PA was not there with Mr Cameron. When we asked his PA, he said that Mrs Cameron had asked him not to come to work on that day. When the PA asked her why, she said, 'I want to surprise Mr Cameron and it's personal.' She even gave him money. After hearing the story, we came to the conclusion that Mrs Cameron was involved in this case. While speaking to Mrs Cameron's maid, it was very sure that Mrs Cameron was greedy for money. Mrs Cameron had her own mansion. We investigated the neighbourhood near Mrs

Cameron's mansion. The guy who was living opposite to her mansion said that at night, he had seen a guy coming to her mansion when she was alone and leaving the mansion at midnight. O n the other side, Jake texted me to come to his house. Eric and I went to Jake's house. At his house, Beau and Jake were sitting in front of the computer. Beau showed me a video of Jacob dropping a bomb. After he dropped the bomb, we couldn't see anything other than smoke. Jake took out a pen drive from his pocket and showed us another video. We were all very shocked to see it.

Chapter 10

The second trial

In the courtroom, there was the judge, us, the plaintiff, Mrs Cameron, Mr Cameron, Lucas, Jacob, Daniel, Lincoln, Mathew, and some other people . The judge explained what happened in the last trial. The p laintiff was the first one to speak.

My Sawyer said, ' There are only six people who entered the special room. In those six, Miss Ava was shot dead. The last one who was there in the room was Mr Cameron. The place is very secured. Other than Mr Cameron, no one could have known where the door and the camera was. How will the culprit kno w there was a camera and door? Who could open the door other than Mr Cameron? All the security guards were gone. W ithout Mr Cameron's order, the security guards don't go anywhere. Mr Cameron must be the one who asked the security to go out and kill miss Ava.'

Jake stood and said, 'Objection your honour, why would my client kill his maid who was loyal to him for 15 years? My client believed in M iss Ava and that is the reason why he took M iss Ava with him to the special room while making the business deal.'

Mr Sawyer said, 'S o who is the real culprit if it's not Mr Cameron?'

I said, 'T he real culprit is Jacob, Mrs Cameron, and Lucas. Here is the evidence against them but before watching the evidence, I would like to bring a witness to the court'

The judge said, 'Proceed.'

The neighbour of Mrs Cameron came to the court. He said to the judge, 'Jacob has been sneaking into the mansion at night . For two years, I have been watching him at night. H e comes and leaves the mansion at midnight.'

The judge, after hearing my witness, went through the evidence which I gave him. There was a video of Jacob dropping the bomb and the next video was completely dark. A guy had a gun in his hand but we couldn't see his face. He was aiming at Mr Cameron but because of the smoke, he didn't see Miss Ava in front of Mr Cameron so when he sho t the bullet, it hit Miss Ava and she died. Soon after shooting, the guy ran towards another exit door. He opened the door. A ll the other three people were trying to figure the way out so when he reached the door, they ran out. No one other than Mr Cameron and Jacob knew about the door. There was another evidence which is that a money transaction happened between Jacob, Mrs Cameron, and Lucas. Mrs Cameron and Jacob transferred money to Lucas' account. It was a large sum of money. H alf was paid by Mrs Cameron and the other half was paid by Jacob. The j udge understood that Mrs Cameron and Jacob were secretly in a relationship. They wanted to kill Mr Cameron to get his properties . If Mr Cameron died , the whole property would go to Mrs Cameron. All the evidence was against them.

The judge said, ' Arrest Mrs Cameron and Jacob. The court finds Mr Cameron not guilty. Section 302, a life sentence for Mrs Cameron and Jacob for attempt of murder. Lucas should be black listed and I give him a four-year sentence in jail.'

I was very happy that we won the case. I hugged Jake but the happiness was very short. Jacob took a gun and pointed the gun at me. He shouted at me saying, ' Y ou ruined my life.' I was scared. I closed my eyes. I heard a shooting sound but I couldn't feel the pain . The police arrested Mr Jacob and took him. When I opened my eyes, I saw that Jake was sho t and he was bleeding. The bullet had been shot in his chest. When Jacob shot me, Jake tried to save me but instead, he got shot. We took Jake to the hospital. H e was in a critical state and there was a lot of blood loss. The doctors took him to the emergency ward . I stayed in the hospital, crying while he was undergoing surgery. Thank G od Jake's blood group was B positive. I got a blood donor fast . It took three weeks for him to recover but he was not still fully recovered. He was restricted from doing the job which strained him so much and he could not carry weight objects. I always prepared food from home till he got discharged from the hospital. After Jake came home, I hugged him and cried. I knew he cared about me but I never thought he would sacrifice his life for me . When he was in the hospital after the surgery, I went to meet him. I was controlling my tears when he was l ying in the hospital bed. The only sentence he said to me was, ' I t's okay if I die because I kissed you.' This sentence always comes to my mind. After fully recovering, he came back to work . He was my life.

The next step which we took was a really big step. His next client was in Paris . I knew how useful this new case will be and how much I will miss him. It was a big opportunity for him to prove himself and I trusted him a lot.

Chapter 11

Long- distance relationship

He had to go to Paris next week. He didn't want to leave me but I knew how important his career was so I asked him to go. One week went by. We stayed together and had fun . The next day was his flight. I went with him to the airport. I didn't want to cry while he was going. I controlled my tears and hugged him.

Jake said, ' I'm really going to miss you while I'm away, baby.'

I rested my head against his shoulder, hearing his heart beat. 'Why is your heart beating so fast.'

He smiled at me and said that this is what you really make me feel. He squeezed me a little tighter like he was trying to make me feel warmer and safe. I always felt safe in his arms.

Jake said, 'What are you thinking about?'

I said, ' I'm thinking about how much I'm going to miss you.'

There was an announcement from the cabin for the passengers. I knew it was time for him to go.

Jake said, ' A lright we... Take care of yourself, baby.'

He kissed gently on my forehead and went to his flight. The n ext few months were boring. I missed him so much . He sent me gifts. W e often F aceT imed. Our work got heated up. A new head came to our law firm. He was harsh , strict, and a head weighted person. He never showed any respect . Jake was busy working and I was also busy working. The time we both spent together became very less. Three months went by like this. I got a va cation. I missed my parents very much so I called them and asked whether we could meet up in LA but they said they were busy then and maybe we could meet some other time. I was worried. It had been years since I saw them. I thought that maybe for this va cation, I could go to Paris. I missed him a lot. I called him and told him that I was coming to Paris. H e was very happy to hear that and he said there is a surprise for me in Paris.

Chapter 12

Paris I'm in love

I took a flight to Paris. I was very eager to visit him. He was waiting for me at the airport. We went to his house where he was currently staying. He told me to take rest and get ready. I asked him where we were going. He said that it was a surprise with a naughty smile o n his face. I took a nap and got ready in the evening. He was waiting for me near the door. He wore a suit. He looked very attractive. H e had a bouquet of lilies in his hand. He gave me the bouquet and took a car for rent. He had a smile o n his face during the whole drive. H e stopped near a place. H e looked at me and winked. It was a fancy rooftop restaurant. He had reserved a seat for us . From our table, there was a clear view of the Eiffel T ower. I t was the best. We ate, we spoke, we he ld hands, and were enjoying the night view of the Eiffel T ower. It was a romantic date. In t he next few days, we visited many places like the Louvre Museum, the Arc de Triomphe, and we ate the famous food in Paris like Baguettes, Macarons, and Eclairs. We went and took lots of photos together. And obviously, we shared very pleasurable moments together. He carried me to his bed but I was very nervous. He knew that I was nervous.

Jake asked, ' W hy?'

I said, ' W ell, you know, I've never been with anyone... '

Jake replied, 'O h... I see.'

He kissed me gently o n my forehead.

Jake said, ' I only want to hear my name coming out from your lips tonight.'

He started kissing me on my lips and after a few seconds, he looked at me.

I said, 'Say any good thing about me?'

He said, 'Y ou can easily turn me on.'

I said, 'W ow, that's not very romantic. Your compli ment is that I make you feel horny all the time?'

Jake said, ' No, it's that you're always beautiful. And the best part is that you're not even trying or aware of that.'

I said, 'S o you went from "Y ou make me horny" to "Y ou are a natural beauty."

He said, ' I am sure I could do even better than what you make me.'

I said, 'O h really? What do you have in your mind, Mr Jake? '

In a flash of second, Jake was on top of me and was holding my cheek in his hand. He started kissing me while his other hand walked around my body. Each kiss mad e me crave the next one. Each kiss felt magical. He bit my lips and I laid my hand o n his back towards his shoulder, pulling him closer to me. I felt my fingers playing with his hair. His hair was soft, silky, and I put his hand on mine and let him take care of me. I wrapped my legs around his waist. The night was real, passionate, and magical. I enjoyed my va cation with him. I came back to Munich. A fter a few months, I started my own law firm with all the money I had been saving. Jake was so supportive. H e came back to Munich. He helped financially and within a few months, we made our law firm bigger and a success. Beau left his job in Law Resolve and joined our law firm. We were both financially stable and we moved in together. Jake bought a beautiful house for us to live in. It was not just a house. It was a mansion with a swimming pool. We came o n the TV. O ur law firm beca me the number one within a year. We become the powerful couple in our city.

Chapter 13

Unexpected love

Jake always wanted to go for a va cation once in a year and even I liked it. Working all day in the law firm and going for a long va cation once in a year was great. He took me to Bali (a beautiful island in Indonesia). Bali was wonderful. T he people there were very friendly. I have always liked water games since my childhood. In Bali, we went for surfing, banana boat ride, and river rafting which was adventurous. 'Balifly' was amazing. I had never experienced it before. In the underwater ride, we saw many beautiful fishes. I never knew that life down in the water would be nice. We took pictures underwater. I fed a bread piece to the fish underwater. I felt like a mermaid with all the fishes around me. This va cation was amazing with Jake. The day before going back to Munich, he took me to Melasti Beach. The beach was beautiful . We enjoyed the sunset and he ld our hands and walked through the seashore . I saw a yacht near me. I had never been on a ride on a yacht . He said there was a small present for me o n the yacht. He he ld my hand and took me inside it. T he yacht was empty. It was empty with no people. The yacht was decorated with rose petals and lights but in the centre of the yacht, I saw a huge box. He asked me to go and open the box with a cute smile o n his face. I was a bit confused about what was happening. I went near the box. The box was taller than me. I was thinking of how to open the box. I n a split of time, my mom and dad came out of the box. I was surprised and tears started flowing from my eyes. I hugged my parents and turned back to see Jake bending down on his knees with a diamond ring in his hand.

Jake said, 'Will you marry me, Bella?'

I said yes and hugged him. He put the ring on my finger and said ' I love you.' I said, 'I love you more.' I didn't know how I got this lucky. His love is like Christmas.

www.ingramcontent.com/pod-product-compliance
Ingram Content Group UK Ltd.
Pitfield, Milton Keynes, MK11 3LW, UK
UKHW021644190726
13853UKWH00001B/37

9 789354 270536